WHERE is the GREEN SHEEP?

MEM FOX
AND
JUDY HORACEK

PENGUIN | VIKING

For Jenny Darling

VIKING

Published by the Penguin Group
Penguin Group (Australia)
707 Collins Street, Melbourne, Victoria 3008, Australia
(a division of Penguin Australia Pty Ltd)
Penguin Group (USA) Inc.
375 Hudson Street, New York, New York 10014, USA
Penguin Group (Canada)
90 Eglinton Avenue East, Suite 700, Toronto, ON M4P 2Y3 Canada
(a division of Pearson Penguin Canada Inc.)
Penguin Books Ltd
80 Strand, London WC2R 0RL England
Penguin Ireland
25 St Stephen's Green, Dublin 2, Ireland
(a division of Penguin Books Ltd)
Penguin Books India Pvt Ltd
11 Community Centre, Panchsheel Park, New Delhi – 110 017, India
Penguin Group (NZ)
67 Apollo Drive, Rosedale, Auckland 0632, New Zealand
(a division of Pearson New Zealand Ltd)
Penguin Books (South Africa) (Pty) Ltd
Rosebank Office Park, Block D, 181 Jan Smuts Avenue, Parktown North,
Johannesburg 2196, South Africa
Penguin (Beijing) Ltd
7F, Tower B, Jiaming Center, 27 East Third Ring Road North,
Chaoyang District, Beijing 100020, China

Penguin Books Ltd, Registered Offices: 80 Strand, London, WC2R 0RL, England

First published by Penguin Group (Australia), 2004

Text copyright © Mem Fox, 2004
Illustrations copyright © Judy Horacek, 2004

The moral right of the author and illustrator has been asserted.

Text and cover design by Deborah Brash © Penguin Group (Australia)
Typeset in 27/40pt Gazette
Colour reproduction by Splitting Image, Clayton, Victoria
Printed in China by South China Printing Company

National Library of Australia
Cataloguing-in-Publication data:

Fox, Mem, 1946– .

Where is the green sheep?

ISBN 978 0 670 04149 7.

1. Sheep - Juvenile fiction. I. Horacek, Judy, 1961- .
II. Title.

A823.3

puffin.com.au

Here is the blue sheep.

And here is the red sheep.

Here is the bath sheep.

And here is the bed sheep.

But where is the green sheep?

Here is the thin sheep,
and here is the wide sheep.

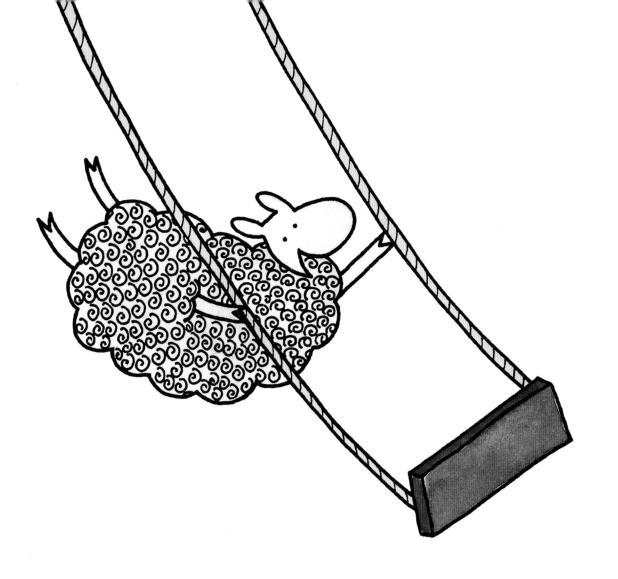

Here is the swing sheep.

And here is the slide sheep.

But where is the green sheep?

Here is the up sheep,

and here is the down sheep.

Here is the band sheep.

And here is the clown sheep.

But where is the green sheep?

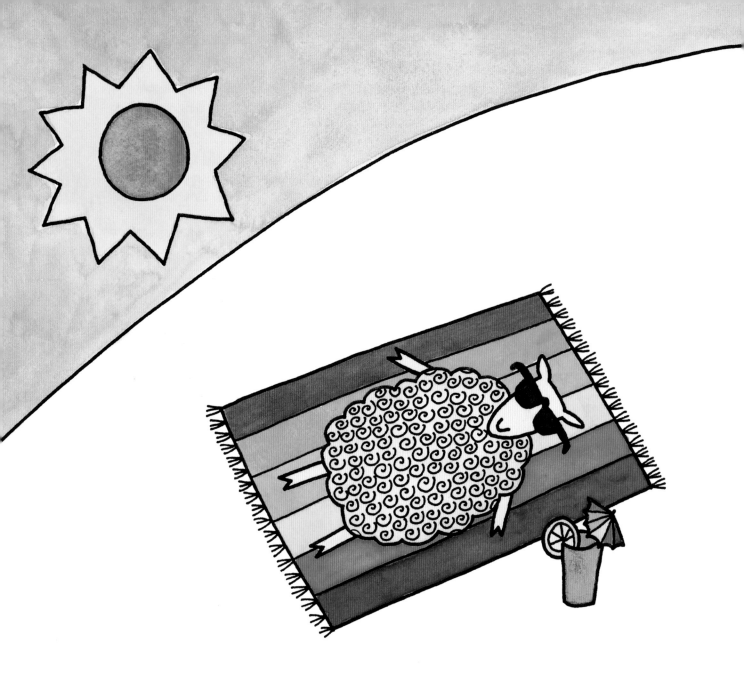

Here is the sun sheep.

And here is the rain sheep.

Here is the car sheep,
and here is the train sheep.

But where is the green sheep?

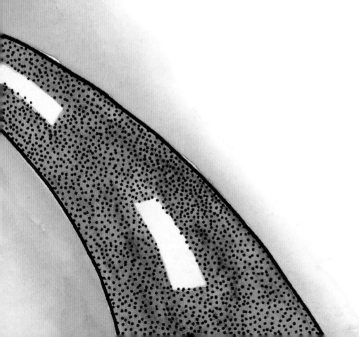

Here is the wind sheep.

And here is the wave sheep.

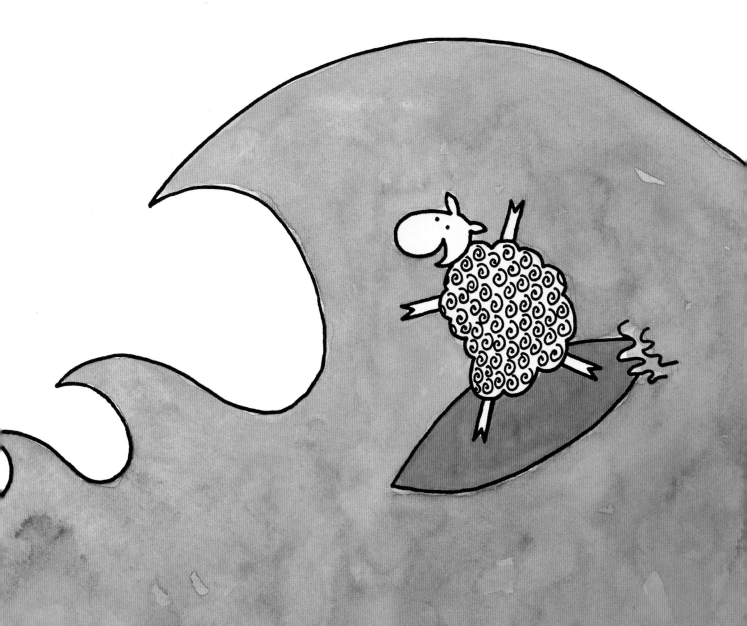

Here is the scared sheep,
and here is the brave sheep.

But where is the green sheep?

Here is the near sheep.

And here is the far sheep.

Here is the moon sheep.

And here is the star sheep.

But where is the green sheep?

Where IS that green sheep?

Turn the page quietly –
let's take a peek . . .

Here's our green sheep,
fast asleep.

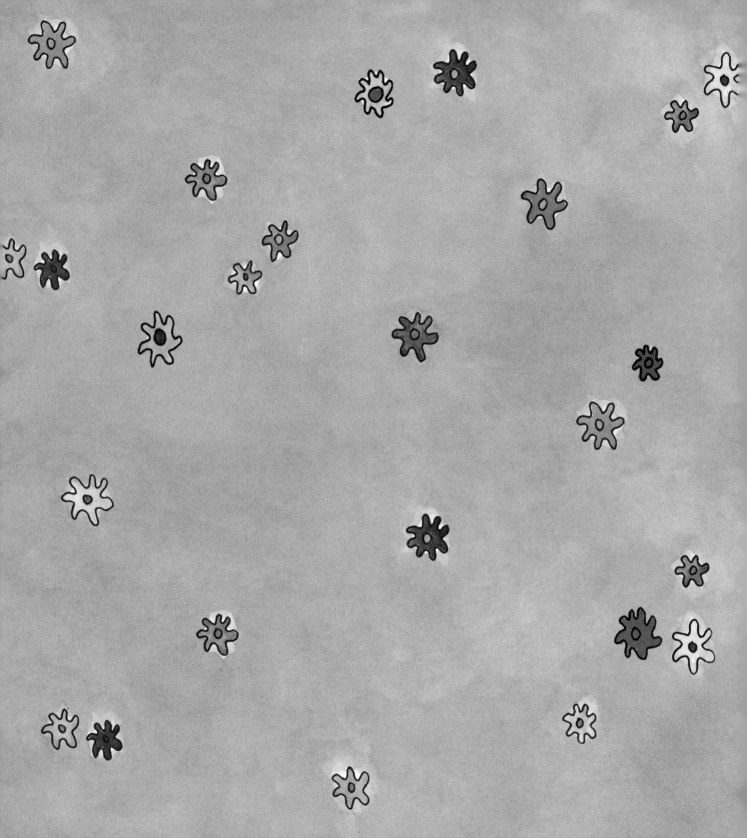